I Love You to the Moon and Back

words by
Susanna Leonard Hill

pictures by
Kim Lawrence

PRECIOUS MOMENTS

sourcebooks
wonderland

I love you to the moon and back.
You make my whole world bright

like sunshine on a summer day
or twinkling stars at night.

Such precious,
sweet perfection—
you are my heart's delight.

Forever and for always,
I loved you at first sight.

With love and joy and happiness
you fill our little home.

And from the first night
you were here,

I've whispered you
this poem.

God's love for you is vast and high
as Heaven above earth,

and just like mine,
His love for you
was there before your birth.

He loves you to the moon and back
with love that only grows.

A gift that keeps on giving—
it's from Him that all love flows.

You'll grow up and explore the world,

find friendships deep and true

with friends who let you be yourself

and always stand by you.

Friendship is like a flower
that blossoms from the heart,

bestowing strength and beauty
even when you're far apart.

Friends love you to the moon and back
through all your joys and sorrows.

You're there for them, they're there for you
for all your shared tomorrows.

You'll always have your family,
a gift from God above,

the people who are always yours
to live with, laugh with, love.

You'll have holidays and birthdays,
maybe vacations too,

family dinners, family games—
your family's part of you.

They love you to the moon and back—
your family's there for you.

They love, accept, support, encourage everything you do.

Perhaps when you are ready,
years from now, when you are grown,

you'll find a special love
and start a family of your own.

And if you're lucky, you will have
a child (or two, or three!)

and then you'll understand
exactly what you mean to me.

You'll love them to the moon and back—
they'll make your life complete.

And you will have the endless joy
of a family life so sweet.

But until then, please
always remember…

I love you to the moon and back.
You make my whole world bright
like sunshine on a summer day
or twinkling stars at night.

Precious Moments®
Copyright © 2020 by Precious Moments, Inc.
PRECIOUS MOMENTS and all related marks, logos, and characters are trademarks owned
by Precious Moments, Inc.
Used with permission by Authorized Licensee, Sourcebooks
All rights reserved worldwide.
Cover and internal design © 2020 by Sourcebooks
Cover and internal illustrations © Precious Moments
Words by Susanna Leonard Hill
Illustrations by Kim Lawrence

Sourcebooks and the colophon are registered trademarks of Sourcebooks.

All rights reserved.

Published by Sourcebooks Wonderland, an imprint of Sourcebooks Kids
P.O. Box 4410, Naperville, Illinois 60567-4410
(630) 961-3900
sourcebookskids.com

Source of Production: Leo Paper, Heshan City, Guangdong Province, China
Date of Production: September 2019
Run Number: 5015963

Printed and bound in China.
LEO 10 9 8 7 6 5 4 3 2 1